Takes the Train

Adaptation from the animated series: Anne Paradis
Illustrations taken from the animated series and adapted by Mario Allard

Caillou was about to take his first long train trip.
Choo choo!
"Yay, here comes the train!" Caillou exclaimed.
But as the train got closer, Caillou felt nervous. The train
was loud and much bigger than he thought it would be.
"Don't be afraid," Daddy said. "You're going to love riding
on the train."

Caillou and his family settled down in their compartment.
Stanley, the train attendant, brought their baggage.
"Are you going very far?" Stanley asked.
"We're going to be on the train for two days,"
Caillou answered.
"Have you ever slept on a train? You'll love it!
It will rock you to sleep."

Caillou looked around the cabin. He was wondering where the beds were.
"I'll take your tickets, please," Stanley said.
Caillou handed them to him. Stanley scanned the tickets.
"We'll be leaving any minute. I'll come back later and tell you the magic words to make the beds appear."

The train started to move. Caillou looked out the window, "It looks like the station is moving!" Daddy laughed. "It's really the train that's moving. But it sometimes looks as though it's the other way around."
On the platform, a boy was waving at the people on the train. Caillou waved back at him.

While Rosie was having a nap, Daddy took Caillou to explore the train. Caillou had to hold on to the wall to keep himself steady.

He laughed and said, "It's like a ride at an amusement park."

Daddy pointed to the symbols on the wall. "Let's go this way. I think we'll find some interesting things."

Caillou and Daddy found themselves in the restaurant.
They shared a triple-brownie sundae.
"That looks delicious," Stanley exclaimed. "Have you seen the whole train?"
"We've seen the bathroom, the kitchen and now the restaurant," Caillou answered.
"You still have to see the best part of the train," Stanley said, "the dome car."

Caillou could hardly believe that there was anything more exciting than a triple-brownie sundae.

"What's a dome car?" he asked.

"It's a car with a roof and walls made of glass. You go up the stairs and suddenly it's like you're flying in a plane."

A plane on a train, thought Caillou.

Caillou gulped down his sundae so that they could continue exploring the train.
"Next stop: the dome car!" Daddy declared.

Caillou climbed up the stairs to the dome car.
Stanley was right. The view was spectacular.
Caillou sat down and watched the clouds float by.
He felt like he was flying high in the sky.

Caillou was having a lot of fun on the train. Soon Mommy said it was bedtime.

Stanley knocked on their compartment door.

"Stanley, we have to go to sleep, but we don't have any beds," Caillou said.

"Let's see if you're ready to say the magic words to make the beds appear."

Stanley asked, "Is it dark outside? Have you brushed your teeth?"
Caillou and Rosie nodded.

"Good! Close your eyes and say, 'sleep, sleep, sleep.'
Then clap your hands three times."
Caillou and Rosie closed their eyes and said the magic words.

Caillou opened his eyes. He couldn't believe it:
the beds had magically appeared.
Daddy lifted Caillou up into his bed.
"Good night, sweet dreams," Stanley said.
"Good night, everyone."
Caillou drifted off to sleep, rocked by the movement
of the train as it rolled along in the night.

Text: adaptation by Anne Paradis of the animated series CAILLOU,
produced by DHX Media Inc.
All rights reserved.
Translation: Joann Egar
Original story: Natalie Dumoulin and Matthew Cope
Original Episode #69: CAILLOU NEXT STOP FUN
Illustrations: Mario Allard, based on the animated series CAILLOU
Coloration: Eric Lehouillier

The PBS KIDS logo is a registered mark of PBS and is used with permission.

Chouette Publishing would like to thank the Government of Canada and SODEC
for their financial support.

Books
Tax Credit

Gestion
SODEC

Bibliothèque et Archives nationales du Québec and Library and Archives
Canada cataloguing in publication

Paradis, Anne, 1972-
[Caillou prend le train. English]
Caillou takes the train
(Clubhouse)
Translation of: Caillou prend le train.
For children aged 3 and up.

ISBN 978-2-89718-463-6

1. Caillou (Fictitious character) - Juvenile literature. 2. Railroad trains - Juvenile
literature. 3. Railroad travel - Juvenile literature. I. Allard, Mario, 1969-   .
II. Egar, Joann. III. Title. IV. Title: Caillou prend le train. English. V. Series:
Clubhouse.

TF148.P3713 2018   j625.1   C2017-941549-2

Printed in Canada
10 9 8 7 6 5 4 3 2 1 CHO20XX OCT2017

MIX
Paper from
responsible sources
FSC® C103304